THE ADVENTURES OF
PETE AND MARY KATE

Martin Waddell has written many books for children, including the picture books *Farmer Duck* and *Can't You Sleep, Little Bear?*, both of which won the Smarties Book Prize. Among his chapter books are *Little Obie and the Flood*, *Little Obie and the Kidnap*, *Fred the Angel*, *The Dump Gang*, *My Aunty Sal and the Mega-sized Moose*, *Cup Final Kid* and *The Perils of Lord Reggie Parrot*. He also writes under the name Catherine Sefton.

D1080033

To the children of
Hare Street Infant School

M.W.

The Adventures of Pete and Mary Kate

Written by
MARTIN WADDELL

Illustrated by
TERRY MILNE

WALKER BOOKS
AND SUBSIDIARIES
LONDON • BOSTON • SYDNEY

First published 1997 by Walker Books Ltd
87 Vauxhall Walk, London SE11 5HJ

This edition published 1998

2 4 6 8 10 9 7 5 3 1

Text © 1997 Martin Waddell
Illustrations ©1997 Terry Milne

This book has been typeset in Plantin Light.

Printed in Great Britain

British Library Cataloguing in Publication Data
A catalogue record for this book
is available from the British Library.

ISBN 0-7445-5416-0

CONTENTS

JUST MARY KATE
7

MARY KATE CLIMBS A MOUNTAIN
19

MARY KATE BUILDS HER HOUSE
39

PRINCESS MARY KATE
59

MARY KATE IN THE PARK
81

MARY KATE, EVERY DAY!
99

"There's no one to play with at Gran's flat,"
Pete told Mum. "No children at all."

Just Mary Kate

Once Pete's mum was very busy, and Pete had to go to Gran's flat every day, for a whole week.

"There's no one to play with at Gran's flat," Pete told Mum. "No children at all. I get bored."

"You can play with your gran, Pete," Mum suggested.

"Gran's too old to play much. She plays for a while, but then she says that she needs to sit down," Pete said.

"Gran will find someone for you to play with," Mum promised, and when Pete arrived at Gran's house the next day, there was someone there he could play with ... that's what Mum and Gran said, anyway.

The someone to play with was sitting on Granpa's armchair. Granpa wasn't there any more, but his chair was, and so was his hat. Gran kept his hat hanging on a hook in the hall, and his photograph up on the wall, and she talked a lot about Granpa.

"This is my friend Mary Kate," Gran said, when Mum had gone. She picked Mary Kate up off the chair and showed her to Pete. "Mary Kate lives here with me. I don't think you've met her before."

"She's just a doll!" Pete said. He wanted someone to play with, not some old doll Gran had found in her cupboard.

"Mary Kate's a very special doll, Pete," Gran said, sounding hurt.

"I don't play with dolls, much," Pete said. What he meant was "at all" but he said "much" because he didn't want to be rude.

"Say 'Hello, Mary Kate' to Mary Kate, Pete," Gran suggested.

"Hello, Mary Kate!" Pete grumped. Mary Kate didn't say anything back. Dolls don't say much, usually, so Pete wasn't surprised.

"My granny made Mary Kate for me, because I had no one to play with when I visited her," Gran told Pete.

This time Pete was surprised. "Did you have a granny?" he asked. It was difficult to imagine Gran having a granny because Gran was so old, and she walked with a stick and had glasses. Pete had a gran and granny, although he had no granpas left.

"It was a long, long time ago, when I was your size," Gran said. "I had great fun playing with Mary Kate."

Pete took a fresh look at Mary Kate, but he still wasn't impressed. The small doll was thin and soft, not much bigger than Gran's hand. She had a funny little rumpled face, and brown eyes that were painted on. She wore baggy dungarees and a knitted jumper which had a few holes in it. That was it. There was nothing special about her at all. Unless...

"Has Mary Kate got batteries?" Pete asked hopefully. He pressed Mary Kate in the middle, but Mary Kate didn't squeak or speak or do karate kicks or anything useful.

"Mary Kate doesn't need batteries," Gran said, laughing at Pete. "She has Mary Kate power all of her own. She'll play with you if you really want her to. You try it!"

"All right," said Pete, taking up the challenge, if only to please Gran and get it over with. He put Mary Kate down on the floor and said, "Play with me, Mary Kate! I really really want you to."

*She had a funny little rumpled face, and
brown eyes that were painted on.*

Pete didn't think anything would happen, and nothing did. Mary Kate didn't move a muscle, because small dolls don't. Mary Kate hadn't any muscles anyway ... she was made of cloth stuffed with rags and horsehair. Pete could see what the small doll was made from, because of the breaks in Mary Kate's stitches.

"Maybe she's bust," Pete said. He didn't care much whether she was bust or not. She wasn't the sort of toy that Pete played with at all.

"Mary Kate played with me, Pete," Gran said. "And I seem to remember she played with your dad a long time ago. Maybe she's shy, or she's been too long in my drawer."

"Maybe," said Pete, not believing it for a minute.

"I know what we'll do now," Gran said cheerfully. "It is time for me to have my sit-down. So I'll go and do that, and you try playing with Mary Kate. Then we'll see what happens."

"I think I might watch TV instead," Pete said.

He didn't want to watch TV, but there wasn't much else to do at Gran's except watch TV or do her old jigsaws, and he'd done them before, all of them. When Gran did play she was good at it, telling stories and making things up, but she never played for very long. Gran always needed little sit-downs, and that's when he got stuck back in front of her TV again. Old people are like that, even the nice ones like Pete's gran.

"Mary Kate will enjoy watching it with you!" Gran said. "Won't you Mary Kate?"

Of course, Mary Kate didn't agree or disagree. She just sat there staring at Pete. It was really annoying. Pete stuck his tongue out at Mary Kate, when Gran couldn't see.

Gran switched the set on for Pete. Then she sat down in her chair with her knitting. Gran started to knit, but her fingers were tired, and before very long the needles stopped clicking.

"Are you asleep, Gran?" Pete asked.

"Not a bit!" Gran said, and her fingers got going again, though the knitting was not quite as fast as before.

"Gran?" Pete said.

"Hi, Pete," said Gran, and she blinked.

"I wanted to know if you were still awake," Pete said.

"Well, I always am!" Gran said. "I just look as if I'm asleep, sometimes."

Pete went back to watching TV. Gran sat in her chair. She had stopped knitting, but she picked up her paper and started to read, with her glasses pulled down so that they nestled on the little red bump on her nose. People with glasses often have little red nose bumps, especially old people who read a lot, like Pete's Gran.

"Mary Kate's tired of watching TV," Pete reported.

"Try switching channels for her," Gran suggested.

Pete had tried all the channels there were. He didn't want to watch any more, but he would still have no one to play with until Gran got up from her sit-down, and that probably meant after she had read her paper all the way through. Sometimes she just sat there holding it, looking as if she was reading, which annoyed Pete a lot.

"It's rotten. I've no one to play with but you, and you're just a silly old doll," Pete told Mary Kate, putting the little doll down on the floor. "Gran says you play games, but you don't!" Pete thought Gran might hear him, but Gran didn't, or if she did, she pretended she didn't, which amounted to much the same thing.

Mary Kate sat very still. If she was annoyed by what Pete had said about her, she didn't show it.

"Gran must think I am silly!" Pete told Mary Kate.

Gran was full of old stories. She made them up all the time. Sometimes Pete thought the stories were fun, and sometimes he didn't. Bits of Gran's stories sounded as if they might have happened, like Gran and Granpa once living on a boat, but Pete thought the exciting bits, like Gran catching alligators with a boat hook for Granpa to cook, might not be true. He could never be quite certain whether she was making things up or not.

"I don't want to sit on the floor watching TV all day long," Pete told Mary Kate, flicking the flicker again.

There was news and a programme about hats and some fat men wrestling and a lady talking about flowers and some cartoons, but Pete didn't want to watch anything, even the cartoons. Sometimes when he was at Gran's house it felt as if he had watched cartoons all day, and you can have too much of a good thing, even cartoons.

"I don't like cartoons. I want something interesting to happen. I need to play games," Pete told Mary Kate. "I am bored!"

Then, at long long long last, something interesting happened...

Mary Kate stirred.

I must be dreaming! thought Pete.

Mary Kate stood up.

This can't be happening! thought Pete.

Mary Kate stretched her doll arms and doll legs.

This is happening! thought Pete and then...

Mary Kate spoke to Pete!

"I'm bored too, Pete," Mary Kate said. "Let's play!"

MARY KATE CLIMBS
A MOUNTAIN

"I thought Mary Kate playing with me was just one of your stories!" Pete told Gran. "But it isn't! Mary Kate says she wants to play games."

"Good!" Gran said, looking up from her paper. If she was surprised, she didn't show it. Pete was the one who was surprised, and Pete wasn't just surprised ... he was amazed!

"What games will we play?" Pete asked.

"Better ask Mary Kate," Gran said, and she disappeared back inside her paper.

"I don't believe this!" Pete told Mary Kate. "I thought you were one of Gran's pretend stories!"

"I'm not anyone's story," Mary Kate said, sounding a little insulted. "I'm me!"

Mary Kate walked round Pete, and took a good look. It was a long walk for someone Mary Kate's size and there was a lot of Pete to look at. Pete was quite small as little boys go, but compared to Mary Kate Pete was gi-normous, almost mega-gi-normous in fact.

"You are very big, Pete," Mary Kate said, sounding worried.

"Mum thinks I'm small-ish," said Pete.

"That's how all mums think," Mary Kate said. "It comes of being Mum-size. I'm not Mum-size. I'm Mary-Kate-size, and Mary-Kate-size is quite small ... so that makes you very big. But not too big yet, I suppose."

"Too big for what?" Pete asked.

"Too big to play with," Mary Kate said. "Like your gran. I used to play with your gran, but I don't play with her any more.

She's too big now to play games with me."

"Gran told me that," Pete said. "But I thought she was making it up."

"We'll play by ourselves, and we won't disturb her," Mary Kate said.

"What game will we play first?" Pete asked Mary Kate.

Mary Kate thought for a bit, and she turned and looked all around Gran's sitting-room. Pete watched her hopefully. He'd looked all around the room himself, and he hadn't found anything. Pete hoped that Mary Kate would, otherwise it would be just watching TV and playing with Gran's jigsaw puzzles. There had to be something better than that.

"Let's climb Armchair Mountain!" Mary Kate said.

They were both down on the floor beside Armchair Mountain.

Looking up at the mountain, Pete felt he was smaller than small, almost as small as Mary Kate was ... at least a part of Pete believed he was Mary-Kate-small, looking up at a mountain. Another part of Pete knew quite well that he wasn't, and went back to being big Pete again ... big by Mary Kate standards that is. It was all a bit confusing so Pete didn't bother too much about it. He was much more interested in climbing the mountain Mary Kate had pointed out to him than wondering about being too big to do it.

"We need ropes to climb," Mary Kate said. "It's a huge mountain, and very dangerous, and there isn't a lot to cling on to."

Pete looked around the room.

"Mary Kate wants to climb Armchair Mountain!" he told Gran.

"What mountain?" asked Gran, looking up. "I didn't know there were any mountains in here!"

"Armchair Mountain is Granpa's armchair," Pete explained. "If you are Mary Kate's size, it's a very big mountain."

"Good idea!" said Gran.

"Mary Kate says it is dangerous, because there isn't a lot to cling on to," Pete said. "We might need a rope to climb it, but we haven't got one!"

"Use my wool," Gran said, and she gave Pete a ball of wool from her basket.

"We might need other things," Pete told Gran.

So Pete and Gran made a list of things they might need for climbing a mountain, and Pete helped Gran to collect all the things.

*   *   *

CLIMBING KIT FOR PETE AND MARY
KATE'S ARMCHAIR MOUNTAIN EXPEDITION
- one handkerchief tent (two persons)
- two emergency ration packs
- one flag to stick on top of the mountain.

"I've got all the things that we need now," Pete told Mary Kate.

"Tell your gran 'thank you' from me," Mary Kate said, and Pete did.

"No bother!" Gran said. "I hope you and Mary Kate have great fun, but look out for Big Mountain Bears, just in case."

"Are there Big Bears on Armchair Mountain?" Pete asked. "Real bears, not like my bears at home?" Pete's bears were Bunkum and Retep (Retep is "Peter" spelled backwards). They were tea-party-on-the-sofa-soft-living-bears from a shop. Pete thought real Big Mountain Bears might be rougher and tougher.

"You never know with Big Mountain Bears," Gran said. "There might be."

"Really Big Bears?" Pete feeling worried about it. He wasn't sure if he wanted to tackle a Big Mountain Bear.

"Could be," said Gran. "How should I know? I've never been up that mountain. But I'm sure you can chase off the bears, if they're there. All you have to do is shout out BEARBOO and the Big Bears run away."

Pete asked Mary Kate if she thought that they could BEARBOO the Big Bears, and Mary Kate said she thought that they could. Mary Kate wasn't scared of Big Bears, and so Pete wasn't either.

Pete divided their climbing kit up so that it was fair. Mary Kate carried the flag stuck in the back of her trousers and Pete carried the rest, because Pete was biggest and could carry more than Mary Kate, and anyway Pete was the one with the pocket that the kit went into.

"One end round me, and one end round you!" Mary Kate told Pete, handing him the rope. Pete could tie his own knots because Mum had taught him how to, so Pete tied the knots for both of them. Mary Kate wasn't much good at knots, but Pete hadn't time to teach her just then.

Mary Kate started to climb up Armchair Mountain, and Pete climbed below, holding on to the end of the rope.

"This is the highest mountain in all of this land!" Mary Kate shouted down to Pete.

"What about Everest?" said Pete. "Dad says that's the highest mountain there is."

"Everest isn't in this land," Mary Kate said. "This is Sitting-Room Land, where I live, so I ought to know."

"This is the highest mountain in all of this land!"
Mary Kate shouted down to Pete.

They climbed up and up, till they reached Arm Rest Ridge.

"Let's camp here for the night, Mary Kate!" Pete suggested. That's what they did. They used Pete's handkerchief-tent. Pete fixed one corner of the handkerchief-tent to the button on the back of the chair, and spread the other three corners out. They could just about both go inside.

"It's time we ate some of our rations!" Mary Kate said.

"They are for emergencies," Pete told her.

"I'm hungry," Mary Kate said. "That is an emergency!"

So Mary Kate ate one of the sweeties Gran had given Pete for emergency rations. Pete ate one as well, and they put the other two back in the ration pack in Pete's pocket.

They slept for hours in their tent. The only noise was the howling of wolves on the sides of the mountain, but there weren't bears about, big or small, so Gran was wrong. Pete knew there weren't Big Bears because both he and Mary Kate kept a look-out for bear tracks. Mary Kate thought the Big Bears might have left Sitting-Room Land and gone off to live in Gran's bathroom, because Big Bears like eating toothpaste. That's why the toothpaste tubes in Gran's flat were all bendy. Mary Kate told him the Big Mountain Bears squeezed Gran's toothpaste with their big paws but Pete didn't know if it was true.

"Today we climb right to the top!" Pete told Mary Kate the next morning. "It must be today, or we'll run out of rations."

They climbed on and on and then...

"Made it!" said Pete.

They stood on the top of the mountain, looking down at Carpet Valley below.

"More food now!" Mary Kate said, when they'd planted the flag.

So they ate up the rest of the rations, and Pete put the wrapping papers back in his pocket so they wouldn't mess up Gran's clean floor.

"I like it here," Mary Kate said, but that was because Mary Kate wasn't keeping a look-out, and she hadn't noticed the danger. Pete was in charge of look-out, and he saw the danger at once.

"The sky has gone black so that means there's a storm coming!" Pete told Mary Kate. "We can't pitch our tent here because it will blow off the mountain, and we would be frozen to death if it snows. And we can't climb back down because there isn't time."

"We'll have to jump off the top of the mountain to the valley below!" Mary Kate told Pete.

"It looks a big drop!" Pete said.

It was Mary Kate who thought of making the parachute, and she told Pete all about it.

Pete made Mary Kate a parachute out of the handkerchief-tent. He tied a different bit of wool on to each corner of the handkerchief, and then he tied them all on to Mary Kate's waist, so in the end Mary Kate looked like a small bundle of wool.

"Be careful you don't hurt yourself," Pete told Mary Kate.

"I'm made of soft stuff!" Mary Kate said. "I don't break!"

Mary Kate jumped. She landed down in Carpet Valley, with a bit of a bump, but it was all right. It was such a soft bump that Gran didn't notice.

Pete stood up to jump off the top of the mountain, down miles and miles and miles to the valley.

"Look out down below!" Pete shouted, and that made Gran look up from her paper at last. She saw Pete standing on the arm of Granpa's armchair.

"Be careful, Pete," said Gran, getting up from her chair. "You could fall."

Gran lifted Pete down from the chair.

"We climbed Armchair Mountain," Pete explained. "There weren't any Big Bears but there was a storm coming and snow and we'd run out of rations and Mary Kate had to parachute off down to Carpet Valley."

He showed Gran Mary Kate and the handkerchief-tent-parachute, tied on with wool.

"You've made quite a mess of it!" Gran said, running her hands through the wool. There were lots of knots in it, and tangles, left over from being a tent and a parachute and a climbing rope.

"You said we could use it for ropes when we were climbing the mountain," Pete said.

"I didn't know it was going to be part of a parachute too," Gran said. "And you can tell Mary Kate that!"

"It wasn't my idea," Pete said. "It was Mary Kate's."

"Well, perhaps you and Mary Kate can roll the wool back into a ball for my knitting," Gran said.

Pete whispered what Gran had said to Mary Kate.

"Mary Kate says she can't do things when you are looking!" Pete told Gran.

"I didn't hear her say that!" Gran said. "She was never so fussy before!"

"Well, she did," said Pete. "You're grown up, so she can't do things like putting wool back into ball-shape while you are sitting there watching."

"That's too bad," Gran said. "I suppose we'll just have to do it ourselves."

In the end Gran and Pete re-rolled all the wool and put Mary Kate back on the chair for a sleep, because she felt tired. Gran read Pete his story and then they went for a walk and Gran got some sausages and then Mum came to take Pete home.

"Don't wake Mary Kate!" Pete said, when Mum went to sit down.

"I wouldn't dream of disturbing Mary Kate!" Mum said, sitting on the arm of the chair.

"Then don't talk so loud," Pete said. "If you wake her up, you'll have to tell her a story before she goes back to sleep."

Then Pete went to look for one of the books he kept at Gran's. He thought he could listen too when Mum read it to Mary Kate, and put in any bits Mum skipped out.

Mum sometimes skipped bits when she was in a hurry, but he always knew what they were and made her put them back in. Pete liked all the words to be there in his stories.

"You'll get your story at home, Pete," Mum said.

"I think Mary Kate might be awake," Pete said.

"If she wakes up, Gran will tell her a story," Mum said. "We absolutely haven't time for a doll's story time. The dinner is on, and it will burn! So tough luck, Mary Kate!"

"You seem to like Mary Kate," Mum said, in the car.

"Yes I do," Pete said. "We played a good game." And Pete told Mum how they'd climbed Armchair Mountain together.

"There are Big Mountain Bears in Gran's flat but it's all right because Mary Kate is very brave, just like me. We know how to scare off Big Mountain Bears," Pete said, sounding just-a-bit anxious.

"I don't believe that there are Big Mountain Bears in Gran's flat," Mum said. "Gran makes up things like that, but you don't have to believe her. I don't want you being scared of Big Bears."

"I'm not scared of Big Bears," Pete told her. "I know how to look after Big Bears. You shout BEARBOO and they go and eat toothpaste instead." Pete told Mum all about the toothpaste that was squeezed in Gran's bathroom, which proved there were bears in Gran's flat.

"All right, I give up on the bears!" Mum said. "But make sure you and Mary Kate and Gran's indoor bears don't have such big adventures that you wreck poor Gran's flat and not just her wool and her toothpaste."

"We never touched Gran's toothpaste, Mum," Pete said. "It was the Big Bears."

"Gran said you were jumping off Granpa's armchair," Mum said. "I suppose you blame that on the Big Bears as well?"

"That was Mary Kate," Pete said.

"I hope she didn't hurt herself," Mum said. "Jumping off mountains sounds dangerous to me. I know you wouldn't do it."

"Mary Kate didn't hurt herself because she is made of soft stuff," Pete told Mum. "That's what Mary Kate says."

"I see!" said Mum. "That's very sensible of Mary Kate."

"Mary Kate is very sensible," Pete said. Then he thought for a bit, and he said, "We're doing something very sensible tomorrow, but I'm not to tell you what it is, because it is our secret."

Then he thought a bit more.

"Mary Kate thinks we might need my bricks," Pete said. "But not the Bad Brick!"

"Why not?" Mum asked.

"The Bad Brick might be scared of Big Mountain Bears," he told Mum.

"That's just like the Bad Brick!" Mum said.

So on Tuesday morning Pete took his bricks with him to Gran's but he made a Pete-mistake. He took the Bad Brick!

Mary Kate Builds
Her House

"Did you bring your bricks?" Mary Kate whispered, when Pete arrived at Gran's the next morning. Mary Kate couldn't see any bricks. She thought that Pete had forgotten to bring them.

"It's all right, Mary Kate," Pete said. "Mum has my bricks in a box in the car."

Mum brought the bricks in, in their box. The Bad Brick was there, hiding in the box, but Pete and Mary Kate didn't know it. Usually the Bad Brick lived under the bed, where it couldn't mess up Pete's games, but this time the Bad Brick had smuggled itself into the brick box. That's because Mum put the bricks in the box, and Mum didn't know the Bad Brick *was* the Bad Brick, because Mum never played with the bricks. She told Pete she might like to play with the bricks, but she was too busy. That's how some mums are. They can't help it. They have to be busy because there is so much for some mums to do.

"What's this?" asked Gran, when Mum put the box on the floor beside Pete and Mary Kate.

"Pete's bricks, by special order of Mary Kate!" Mum said.

"Mary Kate didn't say anything to me about it," Gran said.

"Mary Kate only talks to me now," said Pete. "You are too old." Mum grinned, but Gran didn't look very pleased.

"Never mind, Gran," Mum said. "Let Pete and Mary Kate play with the bricks. It means you'll get some peace."

"That's just what I will do," said Gran.

Mum went away, and Pete emptied the bricks out on to the floor.

Pete's bricks were good bricks, big strong ones. They were wooden bricks, but not like the ones that you buy in a shop. Pete's bricks had been made by his dad from wood that was left over when he was building houses.

Pete's bricks were all shapes and sizes and he liked them all, apart from the Bad Brick. The Bad Brick had a bump in the middle. It made all Pete's buildings fall down. That's why Pete kept the Bad Brick hidden under his bed, so the Bad Brick couldn't get in his way when he was house building like Dad.

The Bad Brick thought it had out-smarted Pete, but Pete spotted it at once. That is because he had written "BB" on it in big black letters, so he would always know it.

"This one is the Bad Brick!" Pete warned Mary Kate, and he put the Bad Brick to one side.

"What are you building?" asked Gran.

Pete talked to Mary Kate, then he said, "It's a secret! Mary Kate says we're not to tell you, yet. She says you'll know what it is when you see it."

"That sounds interesting!" said Gran. "But don't wreck the place!"

Pete talked to Mary Kate again.

"Mary Kate says when we've built it we'll show it to you!" Pete said. "But the important bit is that *we* do the building! I know how to build because of my dad."

"That suits me," Gran said. "My building days are long gone!" And she went to the kitchen to put on the kettle.

Mary Kate counted the bricks. She wasn't very good at counting, so Pete had to help her. Pete was a good counter, because he had done lots of counting at home with Mum.

"There are enough for building my house," Mary Kate said, when Pete had finished counting. He had to do it three times, just to make sure it was right. The first time he counted the Bad Brick in, and the second time Mary Kate muddled the bricks up, but the third time Pete got it right. He knew how many bricks there ought to be, so he knew he was right.

"What sort of house are we going to build?" Pete asked Mary Kate.

"A big house with a door and some windows, like your house at home," Mary Kate said.

"Have you seen my house?" Pete asked.

"Gran showed me a picture she keeps by her bed of you and your mum and dad and your house," Mary Kate told him.

"I like your house, but my house has got to be better than that."

"How better?" asked Pete, and Mary Kate told him. Mary Kate wanted a house on an island, so she could swim every day in the sea.

Pete went out to the kitchen and spoke to Gran. "I need a boat," he told Gran. "A boat that can sail, on the sea."

Gran looked surprised.

"I don't think I've got one just now, Pete," she said. "What do you need a boat for? There isn't much need for a boat in this flat."

"To get all the bricks across the Carpet Sea to Rug Island," Pete explained. "My bricks are all on the wrong side of the sea and Mary Kate says we've got to get them across. So what can we use for a boat?"

"I could give you a plastic carton," Gran suggested, but Mary Kate didn't think much of the old carton-boat Pete showed her.

"Well, you find a boat for yourself," said Gran. "Take a look round the flat."

Pete and Mary Kate looked. There were no boats in the bathroom because Gran didn't play any more with boats, and the boats in the bedroom were only Gran's shoes. Mary Kate didn't think they could row a shoe straight, and a shoe wouldn't hold many bricks, and a shoe-boat might sink if there was a storm when they were crossing the sea, and then they would be eaten by sharks.

"We could only carry one brick at a time in a shoe-boat!" Pete told Gran. "It's a long way to Rug Island, we'd be rowing all day."

"Let's look in the hall," Gran said.

They looked in the hall.

"I don't see any boats!" Pete told Gran.

"I do!" said Gran. "Here's a boat that's

been on the real sea!"

And she took down Granpa's hat from the wall. It was a funny flat hat with a peak, and a bit of old braid round the edge.

"A hat-boat!" said Pete.

"Take care of it now, Pete," said Gran. "That boat's very special to me. It used to belong to your granpa."

Pete looked at the hat. It didn't look much like a boat, but it did look a lot like a hat, because that's what it was.

"Would Granpa mind?" he asked Gran.

"Not a bit," Gran said. "I think you'll find this boat can find its way home all by itself!"

"My granpa was a sailor," Pete told Mary Kate. "Now we've got his hat for our boat."

They filled the hat-boat up with bricks and Mary Kate got in on top, so she could spy out the way to Rug Island. What Mary Kate didn't know was that the Bad Brick had somehow smuggled itself on to the boat.

"Get in, Pete!" she said, and Pete got in, and they rowed.

It was a long way from Brick Point to Rug Island, because Rug Island was right out in the middle of Carpet Sea. They had to row past Brazil and New York. That's when Pete spotted the Bad Brick, and threw it right out of the boat.

The Bad Brick bounced and landed on Gran's foot. "Ouch!" Gran said, looking up from her paper.

"You had your foot in the sea," Pete said. "A shark bit it."

"What shark?" said Gran, and Pete showed her the Bad Brick shark with "BB" on the side.

"I'll look out for that one next time I go for a paddle," Gran said. "Where are you now, Pete?"

"Here!" Pete said, looking up from the floor. He was on the blue bit of the carpet, because that was the sea, and just sailing round the green and white bit.

"That looks like the Cape of Good Hope," Gran said. "Your hat-boat has been there before. There used to be lots of storms down that way, according to Granpa, so tell Mary Kate to keep a look-out."

Pete told Mary Kate, and there *were* rough seas as they rounded the Cape of Good Hope. Mary Kate fell right out of the boat. Pete got her back in and it was all right. The Bad Brick shark almost ate Mary Kate, but Pete rescued her and scolded the Bad Brick.

"The shark didn't eat Mary Kate!" Pete told Gran. "She fell right in but I rescued her."

"You must have been brave," Gran said.

"We've got our boat to Rug Island," Pete

*There were rough seas as they rounded
the Cape of Good Hope.*

told Gran. "It's a very good island."

"Good," Gran said. "Look out for Big Bears just the same!"

"There are no Big Bears here!" Pete said. "You said they were all Mountain Bears. And Armchair Mountain is over there and we are over here and the sea comes in between and the Big Bears can't swim over the sea."

"Well, that's a relief," Gran said. "But keep a good look-out just in case."

Mary Kate whispered something to Pete.

"Mary Kate says you've got to go out of the room now," Pete told Gran. "Mary Kate says you're not to see what we've built till it's finished."

Gran thought for a bit.

"Tell Mary Kate I'll sit where I am, but I'll close my eyes and not look," Gran told Pete. "I somehow feel it is safer that way."

"Why?" Pete asked.

"All sorts of things happen on islands!" said Gran.

"Can I have a pencil and paper?" asked Pete.

"What for?" asked Gran.

"We've got to make plans," Pete said.

Gran gave Pete some paper and a pencil, and Pete made plans, just like this:

Mary Kate and Pete got all the bricks to the island and Pete helped Mary Kate build her house, because Mary Kate was too small to lift up the bricks by herself. Pete knew how to build houses because his dad spent all his time building houses, though his bricks were bigger than Pete's. The houses Pete's dad built were bigger as well. They were houses for people to live in, not dolls.

Then Mary Kate's house wall fell down.

Pete knew what it was. The Bad Brick had crept into the wall. The Bad Brick had a big bump in the middle. The Bad Brick made any wall it was in wobble.

Pete took the Bad Brick out and they built the house all over again.

"This is Mary Kate's house," Pete told Gran. "That's our surprise! If you look through the door you can see her inside it."

"To look right inside I'd have to get down on the floor," Gran pointed out.

"That isn't a floor. It's the sea!" Pete said, and he thought for a bit.

"You'll just have to swim," Pete told Gran. "I don't think you'd fit in our boat."

"You did," said Gran.

"That's because I'm special," said Pete. "I can make myself small when I want to, just like Mary Kate."

"I'm so big that I can walk over your sea," Gran decided, and that's what she did. She walked over to Rug Island and looked down inside Mary Kate's new house.

"You couldn't look in if there was a roof," Pete said.

"That's true," said Gran.

"Mary Kate says if there isn't a roof, she will get wet when it rains," Pete said. "What can we use for a roof? I want a good roof like my dad makes."

So Gran found Pete a magazine and Pete put the magazine-roof on the house, where Mary Kate sat underneath it.

"Finished!" said Gran. "Now can I go back to my chair?"

"Mary Kate says you can go," Pete said.

"What else does Mary Kate say?" Gran asked Pete.

"Mary Kate says 'thank you very much for my roof'," Pete said.

So that was all right.

Gran went back to her chair and she settled down to read her book. Then she got up and went to the kitchen.

"Pete?" Mary Kate said, just after Gran had gone out of the room.

"Yes, Mary Kate?" Pete said.

"My house has no garden ... or flowers."

Pete looked round the room. Gran had some pots and some flowers, so that was all right.

Pete put one of Gran's pots behind Mary Kate's house on the Bad Brick, but the Bad Brick did a wobble and spilled the earth and the flowers out on to the carpet.

"You're a very bad brick!" Pete told the

Bad Brick. Then he got another pot and the Bad Brick spilled that one as well.

"The flowers from Gran's pots look just like trees in your garden!" Pete told Mary Kate. "And the earth looks like earth."

Mary Kate thought that Gran might not mind the pots being poured out on her floor.

They used the Bad Brick to make a seat on the earth in the garden. The Bad Brick was all right as a seat, because when it was all on its own it couldn't make other bricks wobble and fall.

"Let's have a picnic out in your garden," said Pete.

Then Pete went to the kitchen to ask Gran for some juice for the picnic.

"We're having it out in Mary Kate's garden, at the back of her house," he told Gran. "It's very nice there. We've got trees and a seat, and we can look out over the sea."

"What garden?" said Gran.

Pete showed her the flowers and the garden.

"Oh Pete!" said Gran. "What a mess on my floor!"

"It isn't a mess! It is Mary Kate's garden," Pete explained.

Gran put Mary Kate's garden back in the flower pot, and she brushed up the earth from the floor.

"Don't clear up Mary Kate's house!" Pete said. "We need to show it to Mum."

Gran was good. She left Mary Kate's house where it was until Mum came. So Mum saw it, before she took Pete home in the car.

"You shouldn't have spread all that earth on Gran's floor," Mum told Pete. "I think that was a big Pete-mistake!"

"Mary Kate wanted a garden," said Pete.

"Don't blame Mary Kate!" Mum said. "She couldn't lift a flower pot and spill it all out on the floor. I suppose now you'll say it was the Big Bears in Gran's bathroom that did it. I've been in there and I didn't see any bears."

Pete thought for a bit. "It wasn't Mary Kate's fault or the Big Bears, it was the Bad Brick," Pete said. "The Bad Brick spilled the earth on the floor. And that was your fault a bit, because you brought the Bad Brick!"

"I thought it might be my fault, somehow," Mum said.

"Well, not all your fault," Pete said. "It was mostly the Bad Brick. And the Bad Brick was a shark and bit Gran on the toe!"

"All right, Pete," sighed Mum. "We'll blame the Bad Brick. But try thinking up some games for tomorrow that don't wreck Gran's flat. I'm not sure she likes being bitten by sharks, but I'm very sure she doesn't like earth on her carpet!"

"Gran and I put it all back in the flower pots," Pete said.

"What are you and Mary Kate doing tomorrow?" Mum asked.

"It's a secret!" Pete said. "You're not to know, but I know. I told Gran about it. When you come to collect me tomorrow and see Mary Kate, Mary Kate will have changed!"

"How changed?" asked Mum.

"Wait and see, Mum!" Pete said, so Mum had to wait to find out.

Princess Mary Kate

It was Wednesday morning, Pete's third day for staying at Gran's. Mum told Pete in the car that he had only two more visiting Gran days to go. Pete liked playing with Mary Kate, so he wasn't pleased about that.

When Pete got to Gran's, he counted the days himself. "We have three days to go, including today," Pete told Mary Kate and the Bad Brick. "Mum didn't count in today, and today is a playing-with-Mary-Kate day, so she is wrong and I'm right!"

"Then let's start playing!" Mary Kate said.

So Pete asked Gran if she'd got everything ready.

"What for?" asked Gran.

"To get Mary Kate some new clothes!" Pete said. "Mary Kate needs new clothes and we should go to the shops. Mary Kate wants to get out of the flat. She'd like to go shopping."

"I don't remember Mary Kate liking shopping before!" Gran said.

"Well, she does," Pete said. "Mary Kate says her old clothes are rotten old clothes, and she wants some smart clothes like mine."

"Tell Mary Kate her clothes don't look rotten to me," Gran said. "My granny made them for her."

"That means Mary Kate's clothes are very old, almost as old as you are, so she needs nice new ones!" Pete said. "Where can we get some new clothes?"

"Tell Mary Kate I've no money to pay for

new clothes and the shops are a long way away," Gran said. "And it's wet outside, so we're not going out of the flat anyway."

Pete told Mary Kate and Mary Kate was quite cross, because Mary Kate really needed new clothes.

"We'll make Mary Kate some new clothes from things that I've got," Gran told Pete. "Will that do?"

"What sort of new clothes?" Pete asked.

"Perhaps you should ask Mary Kate that," Gran said. "Find out what she would like us to make." So Pete and Mary Kate sat down and had a talk about it.

"Well?" Gran said.

"Lovely ones!" Pete said. "Like a princess."

Gran looked at Mary Kate. "Mary Kate doesn't look very princessy to me," she said. "She looks more like a lady footballer!"

"It's those trousers," said Pete. "Mary Kate says if she had a ball dress and a beautiful cloak and jewels and a crown she would look just like a princess."

Gran wrote down all that Pete had said on a piece of paper, so that they wouldn't forget what Mary Kate wanted.

Princess Mary Kate

Ball dress
Beautiful cloak
Jewels
Crown

"I'm sure we can sort all that out," Gran said. "But Mary Kate might want some other clothes too, mightn't she? Some clothes she could play in, like yours?"

Pete talked to Mary Kate about it and they decided she'd have clothes just like Pete's because even a princess has to have clothes she can play in, Mary Kate said. Pete told Gran what to write down:

New clothes that Mary Kate needs

Mary Kate's Playing Clothes
T-shirt and shorts
with trainers and socks

"I don't know if we can manage trainers," Gran said. "Is Mary Kate sure that she really wants them?"

"Mary Kate is certain sure!" Pete said. "If we're going out, she has to have trainers."

"We're not going out!" Gran said.

"We might want to go out tomorrow, that's what Mary Kate says," Pete told her.

"I'll need to think about how we do that!" Gran said, and while she was thinking Mary Kate spoke to Pete again, because Mary

Kate had thought of something else.

"Mary Kate says she wants some clothes to sleep in so she'll be warm and comfy at night," Pete told Gran.

"Good idea!" said Gran and she wrote that down too:

Mary Kate's Pyjamas

"I wonder what sort of pyjamas Mary Kate had in mind?" Gran said with a frown as she looked at the paper. "We could make her a nightie like mine, if she wanted. Most ladies like nighties."

"She wants pyjamas like mine," Pete said firmly. "My ones at home." He didn't ask Mary Kate. He knew that she wanted pyjamas.

"The nice blue pyjamas I got you?" said Gran.

"Not like those," Pete said. "Mary Kate wants to look smart."

"I thought the blue ones I got you *were* smart!" Gran said.

"My Man U ones are smarter," said Pete.

"Oh well," said Gran. "I know what we'll do. We'll look at the pyjamas in my catalogue."

Gran got her catalogue out and laid it on the kitchen table. Pete brought Mary Kate in to look. Gran had brought the Bad Brick into the kitchen because it didn't like being alone in the other room. The Bad Brick wasn't allowed to play with the other bricks, so it might be lonely, Gran said. Gran said it wasn't a *very* Bad Brick, just a brick with a bit of a bump in the middle.

Mary Kate sat against the salt cellar and Pete sat on Granpa's chair, though he had to have a cushion to bring him up tall enough so that he could see. The Bad Brick sat beside Gran on the table. It was all right because Gran said she liked the Bad Brick, even if no one else did.

"Mary Kate's very excited!" Pete told Gran.

"So she should be!" said Gran. "All these new clothes!"

Gran turned the pages. Pete showed Mary Kate all the pyjamas and Mary Kate chose the ones that she wanted. They were red with *Man U Fan* on the front just like Pete's.

"Tell Mary Kate I think she has chosen just right," Gran said. "They will look very well."

"Mary Kate wants to know what we do first," Pete said.

"We have to find some stuff we can make Mary Kate's new clothes from," Gran said.

They got Gran's boxes out of the

cupboard and rummaged. Gran and Pete pulled lots of old cloth and bits of material out of the boxes for Mary Kate to look at.

Mary Kate was very choosy. She kept putting pieces to one side and saying she needed to look at lots more.

"Princess clothes first!" Gran said firmly. "Tell Mary Kate we can't take all day picking."

"Choose now, Mary Kate!" Pete said.

Mary Kate just sat there.

"She wants me to help her choose her new clothes," Pete told Gran.

Mary Kate and Pete chose some red silk and white lace for her ball dress and an old piece of green velvet to make up her beautiful cloak.

"What about jewels to match and a crown?" Pete said.

"We will tackle those later!" said Gran.

The T-shirt to play in was easy, because they had an old T-shirt they could cut from, one that used to belong to Gran.

"We could make shorts to match from the same stuff," Gran suggested to Pete.

"Mary Kate would like that," Pete said.

Then they started to look for something to make pyjamas from, and Pete found just the thing – an old sock of Gran's with a hole in the toe.

"You'll be very cosy and warm!" Pete told Mary Kate. "We'll put *Man U Fan* on them later and then they will look just like mine." Pete's Man U pyjamas were brilliant, so it wasn't quite true, but it stopped Mary Kate arguing and that was good, because it meant they could get on with the work without Mary Kate interrupting.

"Right!" Gran said, getting out her sewing box. "Now we get busy!"

"What do we do first?" Pete asked.

"First we have to take measurements," Gran said. "We have to be sure that the new clothes will fit Mary Kate."

Pete held Mary Kate up and Gran measured and then they wrote all the measurements down so Gran wouldn't forget them, because Gran said she had a mind like a sieve.

Then they took another look at the catalogue to see the ball dresses and Mary Kate picked the one she liked best. The Bad Brick didn't like it, but nobody paid any attention to the Bad Brick except Gran. Gran told it that bricks have no dress sense and that shut it up.

They spread the silk out on the table and Pete helped Gran mark the shape of the dress on the cloth. After that Gran cut the shapes out very carefully, to make sure that the dress would fit. There was a shape for the front of the dress and a shape for the back. Pete measured the cut-shapes against Mary Kate, just to make sure.

"What now?" Pete asked.

"Now we stitch the two shapes together!" said Gran. Gran couldn't see well enough to put the thread in the needle, so Pete did it for her. He was an Ace Needle-Threader. That's what he told Mary Kate.

"You sew too, Pete!" said Gran.

"I can't sew!" Pete said.

"Yes you can," said Gran. "You stitch in and out, just like this."

Gran and Pete sewed the ball dress together. Gran did the first stitches and Pete did some of the rest while Gran watched, so that he wouldn't hurt himself with the needle.

Then Mary Kate tried on her dress.

Mary Kate was really pleased, and she was even more pleased when Gran added the frills of lace to the cuffs and the hem of the dress.

Gran gave Pete some silver paper.

"You make the crown for Princess Mary Kate," Gran told Pete. "I'll put a hem on her beautiful cloak."

It took a long time, but they did it, and even the Bad Brick agreed it looked good.

Mary Kate tried the whole outfit on together, with some pearly buttons of Gran's that looked just like jewels, and the lovely velvet cloak sweeping round her feet. The cloak was just a tiny bit long for Mary Kate, but Mary Kate said that she didn't mind. Gran told Pete that princesses have long cloaks so nobody knows if they have bony knees. Pete wasn't quite sure if that was true, or just one of Gran's stories. He didn't tell

Mary Kate because Mary Kate didn't have any knees. Her legs were like bent sausages made out of cloth, and clothy bent sausages don't look like knees.

"I feel just like a real princess," Mary Kate whispered to Pete and the Bad Brick.

"Now for the play clothes!" Pete said, but Gran was too tired.

"We'll do them tomorrow." Gran sighed. "I've done enough playing, Pete."

"Mary Kate wants them today! I can make them myself," Pete said, and he did, although Gran cut out the shapes because Pete wasn't allowed to use scissors. Pete wanted to do all the sewing himself, but Gran was afraid Pete might hurt himself with the needle, so they super-glued Mary Kate's seams instead.

Then something went wrong!

"Mary Kate's got no trainers or socks!"

"I feel just like a real princess," Mary Kate whispered
to Pete and the Bad Brick.

Pete said. "Mary Kate wanted trainers and socks just like mine, so we can go out tomorrow!"

"Who said we would go out tomorrow?" said Gran.

"Mary Kate thinks you did," Pete said.

Gran thought for a bit. "We could paint on some trainers and socks," she told Pete, and that's what they did. Pete painted Mary Kate's feet, so she looked as if she had socks and trainers on, just like Pete's but redder, because that's how the paint was.

"What now?" asked Pete.

"Now I'm stopped," Gran said, sitting back in her chair. "Stopped for ever, probably. I've done all I'm doing today. You'll have to sort out anything else Mary Kate needs by yourself."

"Mary Kate wants to play now!" Pete said. "What will we play?"

"You think of something," Gran said. "But tell Mary Kate not to spoil her new clothes before your mum sees them."

That's when Pete had his idea. He told Mary Kate all about it and Mary Kate thought it was brilliant.

When Mum came, Pete handed her a card at the door. On one side it said:

ADMIT ONE MUM ONLY

to

The Mary Kate Fashion Show
Starring Top Model Mary Kate

at

Gran's Flat
TODAY

and on the other it said:

Item 1: Mary Kate's Princess Dress

Item 2: Mary Kate's Playclothes

Item 3: Mary Kate's Pyjamas

All Items designed by Pete and Gran and made from things found in Gran's Flat

"That is your ticket and programme all in one," Pete told Mum. "Please take your seat for the Fashion Show immediately."

"Where?" Mum said.

"Granpa's old chair," Pete said. "It's the best seat in the house."

Mum took her seat and Mary Kate showed off her new clothes on a stage Pete had built without the Bad Brick. The Bad Brick sat on Gran's lap to watch the show, where it could protect her from the Big Bears. They had special lighting effects from Gran's reading lamp and there was a curtain Pete could pull between items. Gran put her CD on and played music, while Mary Kate quick-changed into the next set of clothes.

"I love Mary Kate's beautiful clothes!" Mum said. "Who made them?"

"Cut out by me, sewed or glued by Pete!" said Gran.

"I didn't know you could sew!" Mum said to Pete.

"I can now," Pete said. "But I've got to take care of the needle so I don't hurt myself. I only sew when someone is with me."

"That sounds right!" Mum said.

"And Gran said she hadn't time to put *Man U Fan* on Mary Kate's new pyjamas," Pete told Mum. "Gran said you would probably find time to do it for me."

"Probably," Mum said.

"Mary Kate might need them if she comes to visit our house some day," Pete said. "Mary Kate wants to come. She has no one to play with at Gran's."

"Is that so?" said Mum. "I thought Gran's flat was full of Big Mountain Bears."

"Mary Kate doesn't play with the Bears," Pete said. "The bears are too big, and they all hide in the bathroom all day because she BEARBOOS them."

"Where in the bathroom?" said Mum. "I've been in there, and I've not seen any bears."

"Mary Kate says the Big Bears hide in Gran's shower," Pete told Mum. "They pull over the curtain and hide when people come in to go to the toilet. Mary Kate says the Big Bears hide in there and they drink Gran's shampoo and they play with Gran's soap."

"Don't tell Gran!" Mum said. "She might be scared."

"I don't think so," said Pete. "My gran knows all about bears."

Pete talked so much on the way home that he forgot to think about the next day at Gran's and what they might do, but Mary Kate did a whole lot of thinking as she sat in Gran's flat on the Bad Brick.

Mary Kate knew what she wanted to do, but she couldn't tell Pete until the next day. That's what she told the Bad Brick.

*Mary Kate was up on the window ledge with the
Bad Brick when Pete arrived the next day.*

Mary Kate in the Park

Mary Kate was up on the window ledge with the Bad Brick when Pete arrived the next day.

"There's Mary Kate," Pete told Mum. "Wave to her!"

Mum waved to Mary Kate. "Mary Kate didn't wave back," Mum said.

"I expect she didn't see you," Pete told her.

"I know what it is," Mum said. "She's pretending that she's just a doll, because I am big. If she was just an ordinary doll, she couldn't wave back, could she?"

Pete thought that Mum must be right.

Gran opened the door and Pete bounced in. He went straight to Mary Kate while Mum and Gran stayed talking in the hall. Pete lifted Mary Kate off the window ledge and sat down in Granpa's old chair.

"I want to go out to play like we told Gran," Mary Kate said. "I'm bored with this flat, and I want to go out and play so I can show off the new clothes that you and Gran made for me, Pete."

"Gran?" Pete said, when Mum had gone off in the car.

"Yes Pete?" said Gran.

"Mary Kate wants to go out and play," Pete said. "But she thinks you might be too tired, because Mary Kate says you can't walk very far because of your legs and your stick. So Mary Kate says we don't have to go far, so long as we don't stay inside all day."

"Is that what Mary Kate says, Pete?" Gran

asked, sounding just a bit grumpy to Pete.

"The Bad Brick told Mary Kate it isn't your fault that you can't walk far," Pete said. "The Bad Brick says you are just getting old!"

"I'm not that old!" said Gran.

"You look very old to the Bad Brick," Pete said.

"Not too old for a walk to the park!" Gran said. "I thought the Bad Brick was supposed to be on my side."

Gran took her hat and her coat and her scarf and her stick, and Pete took Mary Kate in his shirt pocket, so Mary Kate could look at the flowers and see all the people. Pete's pocket was big, so Mary Kate sat inside with her head peeping out and her two arms resting on top of the pocket.

"You left the Bad Brick at home," Gran said to Pete.

"It's staying there to scare off the Big Bears," Pete said. "It wouldn't like the park anyway."

"I rather like the Bad Brick," Gran said. "I'm sorry we didn't bring it. Now tell me, Pete ... where are we *not* taking the Bad Brick?"

"Mary Kate wants to go to the swings!" Pete told Gran.

That's where they went. Gran sat on the seat and Mary Kate sat on the swing.

"I want a swing!" Mary Kate said.

"Don't fall off!" Pete warned, but of course Mary Kate did ... straight into a puddle. She was dripping and dirty and wet, and she'd spoiled her new clothes.

"Gran!" Pete said. "Mary Kate's soaked and she's crying, because she has spoiled her new clothes."

"Oh Pete!" said Gran. "So she has."

"I told Mary Kate not to fall off, but she did," Pete said.

They dried Mary Kate as well as they could and Pete blew Mary Kate's nose and told her to be a big girl and not be too upset, because all the dirt would come off in the wash.

"I'm not big. I'm small," Mary Kate sniffled to Pete.

"I think Mary Kate needs an ice-cream," Pete told Gran. "I might want one too."

"I'm not made of money!" Gran said. "You'll have to share one between two." But it was all right. She bought a big one with chocolate on top, so Pete gave Mary Kate some of his. Pete ate all of his neatly because he knew how to lick round the cone but Mary Kate got the chocolate all over her nose.

"Mary Kate is a messer," Pete told Gran.

Then Henry came to the park. Henry and Pete both went to playgroup, so Henry knew who Pete was, but Henry hadn't met Mary Kate.

"Hello, Henry!" said Pete. "This is Mary Kate."

Henry was small and he didn't say much. He held on to his mum.

"Henry doesn't say much. He likes sucking his thumb," Pete told Mary Kate.

"Mary Kate doesn't like Henry," Pete said to Gran. "Mary Kate wants to sit on your knee for a bit, while I play with Henry."

Mary Kate sat on Gran's knee, while Henry and Pete went off to the swings, and Henry's Mum sat beside Gran on the seat.

Henry didn't swing much. He wouldn't lift his feet off the ground. They went on the slide. Henry was too small to slide. He held on tight to the sides.

They went to the sandpit. Pete built a sandcastle, with Henry inside it.

"There must be bugs in the sand!" Pete told Henry's mum. "Henry's all itchy."

Henry's mum didn't seem pleased. She dug Henry out and Gran dusted him off, though Gran said Henry's itches weren't bugs, only sand. Henry's mum took Henry home in his push-chair to give him a bath and get the sand out of his hair.

"I hope you said you were sorry to Henry!" Gran told Pete.

"Sorry what for?" Pete asked Gran.

"You covered poor Henry in sand," Gran said. "That wasn't a good thing to do. I'm surprised at you, Pete."

"Henry's no fun!" Pete told Gran. "He's too small to play."

"It isn't much fun being buried in sand," Gran said. "You wouldn't like it!"

"I would!" Pete said, but Gran didn't argue.

"It might just be time we went home!" she told Pete.

Pete was upset.

"It wasn't my fault!" he told Gran. "It was Henry!"

"That's right," Gran said. "Blame somebody else!"

"I'm not talking to you!" Pete said.

And he didn't. Not for ages and ages, all of the way out of the park and right down the street to the door of Gran's flats and then...

"Oh, Pete!" gasped Gran.

"What?" Pete said.

"Where's Mary Kate?" Gran said.

Pete looked in his pocket, but Mary Kate wasn't there.

"We left Mary Kate in the park!" Pete said. "It was your fault. She was sitting on you, and you ought to have brought her."

"Never mind who is to blame! Straight back to the park is where we are going!" Gran told Pete, and they rushed back to the park and in through the gate and up the path to the swings and the seat where Mary Kate had been sitting with Gran but … Mary Kate wasn't there!

"Look everywhere, Pete!" said Gran.

They both looked and looked all round the playground, but they couldn't find Mary Kate.

"Oh, Pete," said Gran. "Mary Kate's gone off and got lost in the park."

"I don't think she could do that if I'm not with her," Pete said. "That isn't the way Mary Kate works. If I'm not there, she doesn't move or talk or do anything."

"Then where is Mary Kate?" Gran asked Pete.

Pete was very upset because he had lost Mary Kate.

They asked all the mums and dads in the playground and somebody's aunty and somebody's friend, but no one had seen Mary Kate.

"We'll ask the Park Keeper," said Gran. "He might have seen her."

"Have you seen Mary Kate?" Pete asked the Park Keeper, and he told the Park Keeper what Mary Kate looked like.

"Mary Kate is my doll and she's about this big," Pete explained, holding out his hands to show the Park Keeper what size Mary Kate was. "She's a bit wet because she fell off your swing but she didn't get hurt because she is soft and she didn't go in the sand so she hasn't got any bugs."

"What bugs?" asked the Park Keeper, and Gran had to explain.

"Mary Kate is my doll and she's about this big,"
Pete explained, holding out his hands.

The Park Keeper said there were no bugs in his sand.

"Henry got itchy," said Pete. "So that proves there must be!"

"That was sand, Pete, not bugs," Gran said to Pete, and the Park Keeper said that Gran was right.

"Where is my Mary Kate?" Pete asked Gran and the Park Keeper, but they didn't know.

"I'll send her home if I see her," the Park Keeper promised.

"She's lost in the park. We can't leave her here!" Pete said. He sounded sad, because he was sad.

Gran said they had to go home, so they did. Pete and Gran trudged all the way back to Gran's flat but when they got to the door they found Henry's mum standing there holding a bag in her hand.

"I'm glad I caught you!" she said. Pete opened the bag and took out ... Mary Kate!

"Mary Kate!" Pete cried. "Where have you been?"

"She's been for a ride in Henry's push-chair, under Henry!" Henry's mum said. "She must have dropped down there in the fuss, while we were digging poor Henry out of the sand."

"Henry stole Mary Kate!" Pete said, looking round for Henry. He thought Henry might be hiding somewhere behind his mum, but Henry wasn't. Henry was at home with his dad, getting the sand washed out of his hair.

"Now, Pete," said Gran. "Henry wouldn't do that. It must have been me. I must have put Mary Kate down in the push-chair. You should thank Henry's mum for bringing her back to the flat."

"Thank you, Henry's mum," Pete said.

"It's my pleasure, Pete," said Henry's mum.

When they were back in the flat, Pete asked Mary Kate what had happened, and then he told Gran all about it.

"Mary Kate says she meant to go for a ride by herself in the push-chair, but she didn't know she'd get sat on!" Pete told Gran. "But she doesn't mind. She didn't get hurt because Henry is a titch and he isn't very heavy."

"Good," said Gran.

And that's what Pete told Mum when they were driving back home in the car.

"It must have been quite an adventure for Mary Kate," Mum said.

"Mary Kate likes adventures," said Pete. "She gets bored at Gran's."

"Oh yes?" said Mum.

"There's no one to play with at Gran's when I'm not there," Pete said.

"No one but the Big Bears," Mum said.

"The Big Bears have all gone," Pete said. "Mary Kate and I got rid of them!"

"What did you do?" Mum asked.

"We put the shower on!" Pete said. "The Big Bears all got washed away."

"Oh!" Mum said. "Is that how the bathroom floor got wet all over? I thought it might have been a big Pete-mistake."

"Gran said we should have had the shower curtain inside the bath," Pete said. "But Mary Kate says it wasn't our fault because we didn't know the water would run down the curtain and wet Gran's whole floor, so it wasn't a big Pete-mistake."

"I'm sure Gran wasn't too pleased at that!" Mum said.

"Gran didn't mind," Pete told her. "She told me she was glad to be rid of those bears, because they'd made such a mess of her toothpaste."

"I think Gran will be glad of a rest when your week of visits is over," Mum said.

Pete thought for a bit.

"It's my last day tomorrow," he said. "Then Mary Kate will be left all alone in Gran's flat. She'll only have Gran to play with, and she can't play with Gran any more because Gran is too big."

"Are you sure?" Mum said. "Maybe she might play with Gran, just a bit."

"She can't," Pete said. "Mary Kate told me that. That's the Rules."

"Oh well, Gran will be company for her anyway, after you've gone," Mum said. "Gran likes Mary Kate. She's had her a long time, since she was little like you."

Pete thought for a bit.

"You know what I think?" he told Mum. "I think Mary Kate would like to come home to our house tomorrow with me, so we could play every day."

"Do you?" said Mum.

"That's what I think," Pete said. "I love Mary Kate. I want her to come home with me."

"Well I don't know, we'll just have to see what Gran says," Mum told Pete. "But Gran is a bit old. Old people get set in their ways, and she loves Mary Kate. Gran might not want her to go. Poor Gran would be left all alone, without Mary Kate."

Pete thought a bit more.

"You could ask Gran for me," he said.

"Ask Gran yourself," Mum said. "It will sound better coming from you."

"I suppose so," said Pete.

"I know so," said Mum.

Pete decided he'd ask Gran tomorrow, and he hoped she would say he could keep Mary Kate at his house, in his room, with his bears.

Mary Kate, Every Day!

"Ask your gran now, Pete!" Mary Kate whispered to Pete.

"Ask her what?" Pete said.

"About me going to live in your house with you, so we can play every day, and not just when you come to her flat," Mary Kate said.

But Pete didn't know how to ask. He felt very awkward about it. Mum thought Gran might be lonely, with no Mary Kate in her flat to talk to, and Pete didn't know what to say.

"Let's play a bit first, then I'll ask her," he told Mary Kate.

So they played Race Round the World, and Pete won that, because Pete was faster. He had longer legs and he had been in loads of races with his friends. Mary Kate was second. The Bad Brick didn't want to race. It sat on Gran's Knee Grandstand and watched.

"Ask Gran now, Pete," Mary Kate whispered.

"Later," said Pete.

They played Who Can Jump Highest and Mary Kate won. She knocked one of Gran's jugs off the table with her jumping, so Gran wasn't pleased.

"Be careful throwing Mary Kate about in my room like that!" Gran told Pete.

"I didn't throw Mary Kate," Pete said. "She jumped all by herself."

"Then tell Mary Kate to be careful jumping," Gran said. "Tell her I suggest you play something that won't wreck the place."

They played House-Under-the-Table and Roll-round-the-floor-and-hide-away-from-the-Bad-Brick and then it was almost time for Mum to come and take Pete home, but Pete still hadn't asked Gran whether he could take Mary Kate with him to play.

Gran was reading her book, in her chair, with the Bad Brick on her knee, where it could help Gran to hold down the pages.

"Gran?" Pete said.

"Yes, Pete," said Gran.

"Mary Kate says she likes being with me," Pete said. "She says it's been fun while I've been here, because she really needs someone to play with, every day."

"I know," Gran said. "Your mum told me how much you like Mary Kate."

"We've been playing together all day," Pete said.

"Just you and Mary Kate?" Gran said. "You forgot all about inviting the Bad Brick to play?"

"I don't play much with the Bad Brick," Pete said. "It doesn't fit in with the others. Anyway the Bad Brick likes being with you. It likes to sit on your knee. Mary Kate says the Bad Brick spoils our games because it makes things fall over."

"I bet that makes the Bad Brick feel very sad," Gran said. "Poor old Bad Brick. It seems a very special brick to me. It's my favourite Bad Brick."

Pete was getting impatient. He didn't want to talk about the Bad Brick. He wanted to talk about taking Mary Kate back to live in his house. Pete couldn't hold on any more. Pete just burst out and said it to Gran.

"Mary Kate wants to come and live in my house with me!" he told Gran.

Gran didn't say anything.

"Mum said you might be lonely if Mary Kate came with me," Pete said. "But Mary Kate thinks we could come back and see you lots and lots of times."

"When you're gone, I'll have no one to play with," Gran said. "And I've really enjoyed having you and the Bad Brick visit each day."

"Please, Gran," said Pete. "Mary Kate really really really wants to come home with me."

Then Mary Kate whispered something to Pete.

"Gran," Pete said. "Mary Kate says the Bad Brick could stay here with you. Because you might be scared of the Big Mountain Bears on your own, and the Bad Brick knows how to BEARBOO them!"

"You told me the Big Bears had all gone

when you turned on the shower," Gran said. "Remember yesterday? You flooded the bathroom."

"The Big Bears are gone," Pete said. "But the Bad Brick could scare them for you if they came back, couldn't it?"

"Yes, I suppose so," said Gran.

"I think you would like having the Bad Brick living with you," Pete said. "Then Mary Kate could come to my house."

"I wonder what the Bad Brick would say about that?" Gran said. "It might not like the idea."

"I'll ask it," said Pete and he went to talk to the Bad Brick. Pete had to find it first. The Bad Brick had climbed off Gran's knee and was hiding away under the sofa, where it could keep a good look-out for Big Bears … although Pete had told it the Big Bears had all gone.

"The Bad Brick would love to stay here with you!" Pete told Gran. "The Bad Brick says that it loves you a lot because you are my gran and you're so nice to me."

"And I love the Bad Brick too," Gran said, and she added, "if I keep it here, it will remind me of you."

Pete told Mary Kate, and Mary Kate said that she'd have to pack.

"Has Mary Kate got a suitcase?" Pete asked Gran.

"No," Gran said. "But she'll need one for all of her clothes."

"Let's make one," said Pete, and that's what they did.

Gran found Pete a chocolate box. They put all Mary Kate's clothes in it, then Gran wrote "Mary Kate" on the top and fixed it with string so the box would stay shut.

When Mum came, Pete and Mary Kate

were there by the door, waiting. Pete held Mary Kate and her suitcase.

"You're a very good gran!" Mum said.

"I'm all right," said Gran. "I'm quite happy now, because I'll have the Bad Brick to talk to and I know Mary Kate will have fun when she's playing with Pete."

"Thank you for having me, Gran," Pete said. "And thank you for letting me keep Mary Kate at my house."

"Thank you for coming, Pete," said Gran. "And thank you for letting me keep the Bad Brick."

When Pete went off in the car Gran stood at the door with the Bad Brick in her arms. The Bad Brick looked pleased because it really liked being with Gran.

"This is my house, Mary Kate!" Pete said, when he carried Mary Kate in through the door.

Pete took Mary Kate up to his room and introduced her to Bunkum and Retep (which is "Peter" spelled backwards, in case you've forgotten).

"They're Big Bears!" Mary Kate gasped. "You didn't tell me there were bears in your house."

"Don't say BEARBOO!" Pete told her. "My bears aren't that kind of Big Bear. My bears are nice bears, though they don't play like you. They are just ordinary toys."

Then Pete and Mary Kate unpacked Mary Kate's suitcase. Gran had put some sweets in it as well as the clothes. Pete ate some and so did Mary Kate, though Mary Kate didn't eat quite as many as Pete. They put Mary Kate's clothes in the cupboard.

"I'll need a cupboard of my own like yours!" Mary Kate said. "A small one I can reach up to, that sits on the floor."

"We'll make one tomorrow," said Pete.

Pete and Mary Kate went downstairs and Mum made them supper. Mary Kate didn't eat much, but then small dolls don't, and it was her first night in her new house, so she was excited.

They played for a bit and Pete showed Mary Kate all his toys. They were good toys but not like Mary Kate, because Mary Kate was a toy who could play, and there aren't many toys who can do that. Mary Kate said that Pete's best toy was his Space Ship O Base, and the next best to that was the Rubber Ball Bouncer.

"Time for bed, Pete!" Mum said.

"Mary Kate wants to stay up!" Pete said.

"Tell Mary Kate bed means bed *now* in this house!" Mum said.

"Mary Kate says all right," Pete said, and he picked Mary Kate off the bouncer.

"I'm very glad Mary Kate agrees. I just hope she's not too excited and goes to sleep soon," said Mum.

"I'm sure she will," Pete said.

Pete put on his pyjamas and Mary Kate got her pyjamas out of Pete's cupboard and put them on. Mary Kate's pyjamas were the ones Gran and Pete had made for her, which looked just-a-bit like something that might have been cut out from an old piece of red sock. They were cosy and nice and Mary Kate said she liked them a lot.

Mum said that they could put *Man U Fan* on Kate's pyjamas tomorrow. She told Pete that she'd meant to do it, but she had forgotten. Mum said to tell Mary Kate she was sorry. Mary Kate said it was all right and she didn't mind.

"You look very smart, Mary Kate," Mum said.

Mary Kate had her own little bed which Mum had made from a box. Mum set it on the end of Pete's bed, so they could talk.

"Goodnight, Pete," Mum said, and she kissed Pete goodnight and walked to the door.

"Mum?" Pete said.

"Yes, Pete?" said Mum.

"You didn't kiss Mary Kate," Pete said.

Mum tiptoed back and kissed Mary Kate.

"Goodnight, Mary Kate!" Mum said. Then she put out the light.

"Do you want to play now your mum's gone, Pete?" Mary Kate asked sleepily. She had had a long day. She was tired. Small dolls do get tired, even very small ones who can play. It is difficult to know with ordinary sit-about dolls, because they don't do a lot. They just sit about looking the same. Mary Kate wasn't like that. When she felt tired,

Mary Kate had her own little bed… Mum set it on the end of Pete's bed, so they could talk.

her small face looked yawny and sleepy, and she started rubbing her eyes.

"Let's go to sleep, Mary Kate," Pete whispered softly. "We'll play lots more good games tomorrow."

And that's just what they did!

THE

END